APR 1 9 2013

W9-BFM-611

NOPL @BREWERTON
5437 LIBRARY ST.
BREWERTON, NY 13029

Published in 2011 by Simply Read Books
www.simplyreadbooks.com
Text and Illustration © 2011 Boriana and Vladimir Todorov

All rights reserved. No part of this publication may be
reproduced, stored in a retrieval system, or transmitted,
in any form or by any means, electronic, mechanical,
photocopying, recording or otherwise, without the written
permission of the publisher. The publisher does not have
any control over and does not assume any responsibility
for author or third-party websites or their content.

Library and Archives Canada Cataloguing in Publication

Todorov, Boriana, 1966-
    Oliver's tantrums / Boriana and Vladimir Todorov.

ISBN 978-1-897476-67-3

    I. Todorov, Vladimir, 1964- II. Title.

PZ7.T537Ol 2010   j813'.6   C2009-906872-9

We gratefully acknowledge for their financial support
of our publishing program the Canada Council for the
Arts, the BC Arts Council, and the Government of Canada
through the Book Publishing Industry Development
Program (BPIDP).

Manufactured by Hung Hing in China,
August 2011 This product conforms to CPSIA 2008

Book design by Zoë Dissell

10 9 8 7 6 5 4 3 2 1

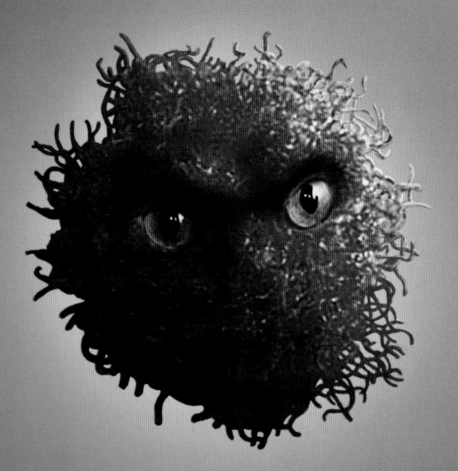

To Alex and Angelina
(you little monsters!!!)

Oliver's Tantrums

Boriana and
Vladimir Todorov

SIMPLY READ BOOKS

O liver wanted to play with his mom.
  "Not now," she said. "Your baby sister needs me."
 That's what she always said. Oliver stomped off, pouting,
to explore the attic. It was full of dusty old stuff nobody wanted.
 "Oi! Over here!" called out a voice from a small wooden chest.
 The lid of the chest was open. Inside were three fluffy balls.
 "Hi, kiddo! We've been waiting for you!" they cried.
 "We're Tantrums," said the yellow ball. "I'm Cedric."
 "I'm Rasmus," said the red ball.
 "And I'm Basil," said the blue ball. "We'll get you
everything you want! Throw us at your mom and you'll see."
 "Great!" said Oliver. He put Basil in his pocket and
went downstairs.

Oliver's mother was tickling his sister Polly.

"Play with ME!" said Oliver.

She tickled him once and then went back to Polly.

"I want to have fun!" Oliver began to cry. A tear trickled down his cheek and fell on the floor. More followed.

"Hey, kiddo," whispered Basil, "don't work so hard! Throw me."

Oliver sniffled, wiped his nose, and took the blue ball out. He tossed it at his mother.

WHOOSH! Basil turned into a monster of swirling water. He poured himself over Oliver's mom.

"Fine! Fine!" she shouted. She put Polly in her crib. Then she began to tickle Oliver.

Basil hung in the air for a moment, then winked at Oliver and turned back into a blue ball.

In the weeks that followed, the blue Tantrum worked really hard. And his splendid water displays had amazing results. Every time Oliver was bored, he threw Basil at his mom and Basil made everything fun.

Life couldn't be better. Until one day …

Oliver's mom charged into the room, covered from head to toe in a shiny rubber suit and wielding a mop.

Oliver threw Basil at her. She disappeared in a wave of water.

"Ha!" cried Oliver's mom, attacking Basil with her mop. When she was finished, all that remained was a tiny puddle and the blue ball.

"I've got to put Polly to bed now," she announced, taking off her mask.

When she left, Oliver picked up Basil. "Mom's figured you out."

"Don't worry, kid," said Basil. "You still have Cedric and Rasmus."

Oliver returned Basil to the chest in the attic and put Cedric, the yellow ball, in his pocket.

The next night, Oliver took one look at his dinner and scrunched up his face. "UGH! I want cookies!"

"Try one bite," his mom said. "Polly loves her spaghetti."

"No! Cookies!"

His mom kept insisting he eat some spaghetti.

"Hey, mate," came a voice from his pocket, "throw me!"

Oliver took out the yellow ball and lobbed it at his mother. WHOOSH! It hit the table, and up rose a monster draped in spaghetti and dripping with tomato sauce. Cedric slobbered and dribbled. He squished and squashed. Then he lurched at Oliver's mother and splattered her with mushy food.

"Ok! Ok!" she cried and slammed the cookie jar down in front of Oliver. "Have it your way."

In the weeks that followed, the yellow Tantrum worked really hard. And his magnificent romps had amazing results. Cedric made sure Oliver got all his favorite treats. Everything was going very well. Until one day ...

"No more treats, Oliver," said his mother.

Oliver threw Cedric, who instantly turned into the spaghetti monster.

"Not this time!" his mother cried. From behind her back, she pulled out a vacuum cleaner and flicked on the switch.

Cedric didn't stand a chance. Soon all that was left was a twitching noodle under the stove and the yellow ball.

When his mother left, Oliver, with a look of dismay, picked Cedric up.

"I don't feel so good," Cedric whispered. "But there's still Rasmus, the red ball, remember?"

"Right!" Oliver said. "I'll go get him."

Shortly after, Oliver noticed some of his toys were broken. "I want new toys!" he demanded. "Polly keeps breaking mine!"

His mom shook her head.

That's when Oliver heard a voice coming from his pocket: "Hey, buddy! It's me, Rasmus. How 'bout havin' some fun?"

Oliver launched Rasmus in the air. WHOOSH!

The floor shook as a monster made of mangled toys grew before their eyes.

"Take cover, boy!" Rasmus shouted.

A rapid round of paintballs turned the walls into rainbows. Rasmus banged drums and blew horns. Oliver's mother grabbed her purse and shouted, "Fine! Let's go buy you a new train!"

"Great!" cried Oliver. Rasmus turned back into a red ball, and Oliver stuck him into his pocket.

In the weeks that followed, the red Tantrum worked really hard. And his crazy capers had amazing results. Rasmus made sure Oliver got all the toys he wanted.

Oliver was on top of the world. Until one day …

Oliver's mother appeared in firefighter's gear, complete with a fire hose, which she turned on the toy monster.

The blast of water was so powerful that Rasmus collapsed. Parts rolled under Oliver's bed, until all that was left of him was a cogwheel and a red ball.

"Sorry, buddy!" said Rasmus. "I'm finished."

But Oliver was not ready to give up his three Tantrums.

Back in the attic, Oliver threw all three balls at the wall.

WHOOSH! WHOOSH! WHOOSH! His Tantrums stood before him.

"You aren't working anymore!"

"Well," Cedric said, "if you jus' put me in charge of these two 'ere,
I reckon I can ..."

"You're joking!" laughed Basil.

"I always work solo, myself," Rasmus added.

That gave Oliver an idea. "This time you'll work together as a team!"

"No way!" they shouted.
"Yes way!" said Oliver.
He put all three balls in his pocket and waited for the right
moment to use them. It came sooner than Oliver expected …

The next morning, Oliver was playing dress-up when his mother came down. She was wearing a suit of armor, too.

"Play knights with me?" asked Oliver.

"No, Oliver. I don't have time. I just thought I'd better be ready, in case, well … remember when we visited your new school?" she asked.

"I don't want to go to school!" cried Oliver.

"You'll like it there," his mother coaxed.

"No, I won't! Polly doesn't have to go to school. You just want to get rid of me!"

He stuck his hand in his pocket and pulled out the three balls. "You don't love me anymore!" he cried and threw the Tantrums as hard as he could. KABOOM! The biggest, meanest monster Oliver had ever seen rose up and charged at his mother.

"ROAR!"

But Oliver's mother didn't prepare for battle. Instead, she lowered her sword and opened her visor.

"Oh, Oliver, that's not true!" she said. "I've just been busy with Polly. I didn't mean to ignore you."

"Really?" asked Oliver.

"Really!" she replied. "I love you."

"ROAR!" the monster howled and struck out at Oliver's mother.

Oliver charged at the terrible Tantrum. "No!" he shouted. "NOOOOOOOOO!!!"

The monster shuddered and trembled and fell to the ground. Within moments, all that remained were a heap of dust and three balls.

Oliver scooped them up and put them back in their wooden chest.

Then he hid the chest in the attic where no one would find it.

Or so he thought ...

The End !